for Avery, Aubrey, Cindy, and David

Pansy in Venice

The Mystery of the Missing Parrot

written by Cynthia Bardes

illustrations by Virginia Best

Published by Octobre Press

Vero Beach, Florida 32960

www.PansythePoodle.com

Illustrations by Virginia Best

Editorial Development by Laura Ross

Art Editing by Aubrey Thorne Carey

Art Design by Cynthia Bardes

PRINTED IN THE UNITED STATES

This book was typeset in Berkeley.

ISBN 978-0-692-34554-2

Paris Daily

all the news you need

Paris Weather
Sunny & Mild

Mystery of Missing Museum Masterpieces Solved!

Huggable Hero
Pansy the Poodle

A Tiny Toy Poodle
solves her second mystery!

Our favorite doggy detective snared a sneaky thief and recovered some very important paintings for the museum here in Paris, France. Pansy was invited to Paris to help because she caught a jewel thief at the Palace Hotel in Beverly Hills, California. What will she do next?

I was packing to go home from Paris when Avery burst into the room. "Mommy, it's the mayor of Venice, Italy! He saw us on TV! A very important parrot is missing. He needs us to help find it. The mayor says it is urgent."

"We need to go!" said Mama. "I will call your father and tell him we won't be home yet."
We finished packing in a hurry. We left the hotel and went to the train station.
We were off to Venice! I was sooooo excited!

Soon, we were on the fast train to Venice
and off on another adventure!
"The streets of Venice are made of water," said Mama.
"Instead of cars and buses, the people take boats!"
I couldn't sit still. The train whistle sang out, *hooooo, hooooooo!*
I sang out *hoooo, hooooo,* too!

When we arrived, I couldn't believe it!
There was water EVERYWHERE!

"Welcome to Venice," said the mayor.
"I have a fast boat to take us to the island of Murano.
That is where Penelope the parrot lived
before she disappeared."

"The most beautiful glass in the whole world is made on the island of Murano," said the mayor. "Signor Lorenzo is the master glass-blower. Penelope the parrot lived with Signor Lorenzo and sang beautiful songs to him all day long. Now, she is missing and he is so sad he cannot work. The glass shops may soon be empty."

"Signor Lorenzo," said the mayor, "I'd like you to meet
Pansy the mystery-solving poodle and her best friend, Avery.
They have come to help find Penelope."

"*Buon giorno* (good day), Pansy and Avery," said Signor
Lorenzo. "I am so sad. My best friend has vanished!"

DO NOT TOUCH OVEN

WATCH GLASS BEING MADE HERE

"I'm so sorry," said Avery.
"Please tell us what Penelope looks like."
"My beautiful Penelope is the color of the sun, with cherry red tips on her feathers and bright green feet. Here is her picture."

"Don't worry, we'll find her," said Avery. "Pansy is very good at solving mysteries. She once caught a jewel thief!"

I wagged my tail and gave him my paw. *Yip, yip,* I said. *Let's get started!*

MURANO GLASS

COSTUMI
COSTUMES & MASKS

CAFFE

The mayor showed us around Venice while I sniffed for clues.

I saw something! A yellow feather with a cherry red tip!
Yip, yip, I barked.

"Ooohh!" said Avery and put the feather in her pocket.

We stopped to eat pizza and the best ice cream ever.
The mayor called the ice cream *gelato*.
"Now let's go to the costume shop," he said. "You are invited
to a costume ball tonight. There will be music and dancing."
"Wow!" said Avery.
I wiggled and jumped . . . I love to dance!

Inside the shop, we tried on lots of fancy costumes.
Then I saw something on the floor.
It was another yellow feather with a cherry red tip!
Yip, yip, I said.
"Oh!" said Avery, and put the feather in her pocket with the other one.

Back at the hotel, we put on our costumes. Avery was a beautiful princess in a shiny pink dress with stars and bows. I was a clown with a pointy green hat and a big ruffle around my neck.

To go to the party, we climbed into a strange boat that looked like a sea monster.
"*Buona sera* (good evening), Pansy and Avery. My name is Giorgio," said the man in the
boat. "This is a gondola and I am a gondolier." As he pushed the boat with a long pole,
he began to sing.
I sang along, *Hoo, yip, hoo, hoo!*

Giorgio stopped the gondola in front of the biggest,
fanciest house I had ever seen.
"This is the palace of Count D'Oro," he said. "He is
the richest man in all of Venice. He lives alone, but every year
he invites all of the people of Venice to a carnival costume ball."

"Welcome to the ball," said Count D'Oro.
"There are lots of yummy things to eat and drink."
"Thank you," said Avery.
I heard music! *Hoo, hoo*, I sang, and I started to dance.

Everyone was dressed up in fancy costumes.
Even the mayor was wearing a funny outfit.

Soon, I was dancing so fast I started to pant. I was very hot!
"Let's go outside," said Avery. "You can get a drink of water from the fountain."

We danced out the door.

Outside, the moon was bright. I spotted something yellow on the ground.
Yes! It was another feather with a red tip!

I woofed quietly and Avery turned around.
"Penelope could be close by!" she whispered, as she put the feather into her pocket.

Suddenly, I noticed a light shining from a window behind me.
I turned to look. There was a PARROT in a cage!
Yip! Yip! Yip!
Avery looked and said, "Let's go find the mayor!"

The mayor, Avery, and I left the party and hurried to find Signor Lorenzo.

We knocked loudly on his door until we woke him up.

"Signor Lorenzo, look what Pansy found!" Avery said, taking out the feathers.

"Those are Penelope's feathers!" Signor Lorenzo cried. "Where is Penelope? Do you know where she is? Oh, please take me to her!"

I yelped and started to run back to the palace.
"Follow Pansy!" Avery shouted.
Everyone started running.

When I got to the window
I jumped up and down and barked.

"Penelope!" cried Signor Lorenzo.
Suddenly, the air was filled with Penelope's song.
Carooo, caroooo!

Count D'Oro rushed into the room. "Penelope, you
are finally singing for me! I have waited and waited . . ."

Then he saw our faces at the window.
His eyes got very BIG.

"Count D'Oro," yelled the mayor, "why did you take Penelope? Stealing is wrong! You have so much!"

"Signor Lorenzo, I am very sorry," said Count D'Oro. "You always seemed so happy when Penelope sang to you. I wanted to be happy and have a special friend, too. I made a big mistake."

"Please do not punish Count D'Oro," said Signor Lorenzo. "I have my Penelope back and that is all that matters."

"I have an idea," said Avery.
"Count D'Oro, why don't you share your big palace
with all of the animals who are alone like you?
You could give them a forever home
and have lots of new friends."

Count D'Oro thought for a moment.
"I'll do it!" he said.
And for the first time, I saw him smile.

Carooo, carrooo! sang Penelope.
"Bravo!" said the mayor.
Yip, yip, I whooped, remembering that I had been alone, too,
until Avery adopted me.

The D'Oro Palace Home for Animals opened with a big celebration.
Penelope and I led the animals into their beautiful new home.

When it was time to go home, I looked at Avery,
my best friend in the whole world, and I felt so happy!
Avery looked at me and said, "I love you, Pansy.
Together we can do anything."